Macbeth

A Shakespeare Story

RETOLD BY ANDREW MATTHEWS
ILLUSTRATED BY TONY ROSS

ORCHARD BOOKS

For the Michaels
A.M.

For Zoë
T.R.

ORCHARD BOOKS
338 Euston Road, London NW1 3BH
Orchard Books Australia
Hachette Children's Books
Level 17/207, Kent St, Sydney, NSW 2000
This text was first published in Great Britain in the form of
a gift collection called *The Orchard Book of Shakespeare Stories*,
illustrated by Angela Barrett in 2001.
This edition first published in hardback in Great Britain in 2002
First paperback publication 2003
Text © Andrew Matthews 2001
Illustrations © Tony Ross 2002
The rights of Andrew Matthews to be identified as the author and
Tony Ross as the illustrator of this work have been asserted by them in
accordance with the Copyright, Designs, and Patents Act, 1988.
ISBN 978 1 84121 344 6 (paperback)
5 7 9 10 8 6 4 (paperback)
A CIP catalogue record for this book is available
from the British Library.
Printed in China

Contents

Cast List

The Three Witches – or Weird Sisters

Macbeth

Thane of Glamis
General to King Duncan

Lady Macbeth

Wife to Macbeth

Banquo

General to King Duncan

King Duncan

King of Scotland

Malcolm and Donalbain

The King's sons

Macduff

Thane of Fife

A servant of Glamis Castle

Two Murderers

The Scene

Scotland in the eleventh century.

When shall we three meet again?
In thunder, lightning, or in rain?
When the hurly-burly's done,
When the battle's lost and won.

First and Second Witches; I.i.

Macbeth

All day, the three witches waited on the edge of the battlefield. Hidden by mist and magic, they watched the Scottish army win a victory over the invading forces of Norway, and after the fight was done they lingered on, gloating over the moans of the dying.

As thunder rolled overhead and rain lashed down, one of the witches raised her long, hooked nose to the wind and sniffed like a dog taking a scent. "He will be here soon," she said.

The second witch stroked the tuft of silvery hair that sprouted from her chin, and grinned, showing her gums. "I hear the sound of hooves, sisters," she said.

The third witch held up a piece of rock crystal in front of her milky, blind eyes. Inside the crystal, something seemed to move. "I see him!" she screeched. "He comes! Let the spell begin."

* * *

Two Scottish generals rode slowly away
from the battlefield, their heads lowered
against the driving rain.

One was Macbeth, the Thane of Glamis,
the bravest soldier in King Duncan's army.
He was tall, broad-shouldered and had a
warrior's face, broken-nosed and scarred
from old fights.

His companion and friend, Banquo was younger and slimmer, with a mouth that was quick to smile, although he wasn't smiling now.

Macbeth's dark eyes were distant as he recalled the details of the day's slaughter. 'A hard fight to protect an old, feeble King,' he thought. 'If I ruled Scotland...' His mind drifted off into a familiar daydream: he saw himself seated on the throne, with the golden crown of Scotland circling his brow...

Suddenly his horse reared and whinnied, its eyes rolling in terror. Macbeth struggled to control the horse, and at that moment a bolt of lightning turned the air violet. In the eerie light he saw three weird hags barring the way, their wild hair and ragged robes streaming like tattered flags in the wind.

Macbeth's hand
flew to his sword,
but Banquo hissed
out an urgent
warning. "No, my
friend! I do not think

swords can harm creatures like these."

A small, cold fear entered Macbeth's
heart, and he snarled to conceal it.
"What do you want?" he demanded of the

witches. "Stand aside!"

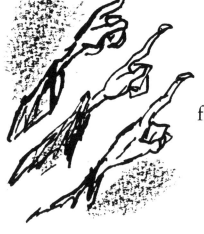

Moving as one,
the witches raised
their left arms and
pointed crooked
fingers at Macbeth.
They spoke, and
their voices grated
like iron on stone.

"All hail, Macbeth, Thane of Glamis!"
"All hail, Macbeth, Thane of Cawdor!"
"All hail, Macbeth, who shall be King!"

Macbeth gave a startled gasp – how had these withered crones come to read his secret thoughts?

The witches turned their fingers to Banquo. "All hail, Banquo!" they chanted. "Your children shall be kings!"

And they vanished like a mist of breath on a mirror.

"Were they ghosts?" Banquo whispered in amazement.

"They were madwomen!" snorted Macbeth. "How can I be Thane of Cawdor? He is alive and well and one of King Duncan's most trusted friends."

"And how could my children be kings if you took the throne?" Banquo asked.

The sound of hoofbeats made both men turn their heads. Out of the rain appeared a royal herald. He pulled his horse to a halt and lifted a hand in salute. "I bring great news!" he announced. "The Thane of Cawdor has confessed to treason and has been executed. The King has given his title and lands to you, noble Macbeth. He has proclaimed you as his heir, after his sons Malcolm and Donalbain. All hail, Macbeth, Thane of Glamis *and* Cawdor!"

Macbeth's face turned deathly pale. 'So the witches told the truth?' he thought. 'Only Duncan and his sons stand between me and the crown! My wife must know of this – I will write to her tonight.'

Macbeth was so deep in thought that he didn't notice the troubled look that

Banquo gave him. The witches had left a scent of evil in the air, and Banquo seemed to smell it clinging to his friend.

* * *

Lady Macbeth stood at the window of her bedchamber, gazing out at the clouds gathering above the turrets of Glamis Castle. In her right hand, she held the letter from her husband, and its words echoed through her mind. "Glamis, Cawdor, King, you could have them all!" she whispered. "But I know you too well, my lord. You want greatness, but you shrink from what you must do to get it. If only..."

There was a knock at the door. Lady Macbeth started and turned, her long black hair whispering against the green silk of her gown. "Come!" she called.

A servant entered. "A message from Lord Macbeth, my lady," he said. "He bids you prepare a royal banquet, for the King will stay at Glamis tomorrow night."

"What?" Lady Macbeth gasped in amazement. "Are you mad?" She quickly recovered herself. "Go and tell the other servants to make ready for the King!" she commanded.

When she was alone again, Lady Macbeth opened the window, and a blast of cold air caught her hair and swirled it about her face. "Fate leads Duncan to Glamis!" she murmured. "Come to me, Powers of Darkness! Fill me with cruelty, so I may teach my husband how to be ruthless!"

A low growl of thunder answered her.

✳ ✳ ✳

Macbeth rode ahead of the King's party, and arrived at Glamis just after sunrise. When his wife greeted him he noticed a hard, determined look in her eyes. "The King sleeps here tonight," he said. "Is his room ready?"

"All is ready…for Duncan's last night on Earth!" said Lady Macbeth.

"What do you mean?" Macbeth asked.

Lady Macbeth moved closer, and spoke in a low voice. "I guessed the thoughts that lay behind your letter," she said. "Duncan is old and weak. His sons are not 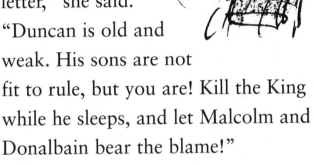 fit to rule, but you are! Kill the King while he sleeps, and let Malcolm and Donalbain bear the blame!"

Macbeth was astonished – first the witches, and now his wife had seen his innermost thoughts. Some strange force seemed to have taken control of his life, and he fought against it. "I will never commit murder and treason!" he declared.

"I will put a sleeping-potion in a jug of wine and send it to the guards at the King's door," Lady Macbeth said quickly.

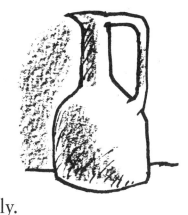

"They will sleep like babes. It will be easy for you to slip into Duncan's room."

"No! I cannot!" Macbeth groaned. Lady Macbeth's face twisted into a sneer. "This is your real chance to be King," she said. "Are you too cowardly to take it?"

"I am no coward!" snapped Macbeth.

"Then prove it!" Lady Macbeth hissed. "Kill the old man and take the throne!"

Once more, the strange force moved through Macbeth, flowing into him from his wife until he was unable to resist. 'All hail, Macbeth, who shall be King!' he thought, and he could almost feel the crown upon his head.

Long after the castle had fallen silent, Macbeth left his room and crept along the corridors. His hands trembled, and the sound of his pulse in his ears was like the beating of a battle drum. 'This is the hour of the wolf and the witch,' he thought,

'when evil spirits roam the night.'

And as the words crossed his mind, a
ghostly glow gathered in the darkness,
shaping itself into a dagger that floated
in the air, shining with a sickly green light.
Macbeth almost cried out in terror.

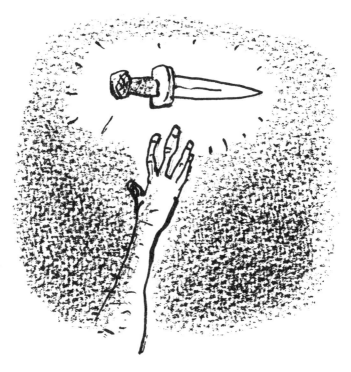

"Be calm!" he told himself. "This is a trick of the mind!" To prove it, he reached out his hand to take the dagger, but it floated away from him and pointed the way to Duncan's door. Blood began to ooze from the blade, as though the iron were weeping red tears.

A bell tolled midnight.

"Duncan's funeral bell is ringing!" muttered Macbeth, and he followed the dagger through the gloom.

* * *

Lady Macbeth also heard the bell toll, and it seemed a long time before her husband returned. There was blood on his face and hands, and he carried two daggers.

"You should not have brought the daggers here!" said Lady Macbeth. "Go back and put them into the guards' hands, as we planned!"

Macbeth's eyes were blank. He shook his head. "I will not go back there!" he said hoarsely.

"Then *I will!*" said Lady Macbeth, and snatched the daggers from Macbeth's hands and left the room.

Macbeth stood where he was, shivering uncontrollably, seeing nothing but Duncan's dead eyes staring. He tried to pray, but his lips and tongue would not form the words.

In a short while, Lady Macbeth came back, holding her red hands up to the candle-light. "I smeared blood over the guards' faces, to make them seem guilty," she said. "In the morning, we will have them tortured until they say that Duncan's sons paid them to kill him!"

Her face was so full of triumph and cruelty, that Macbeth no longer recognised it. He turned away, and caught sight of his reflection in the mirror. It was as if he were looking at someone else – as if he and his wife had become strangers to themselves and each other.

✳ ✳ ✳

Glamis Castle was woken in the grey light of dawn by voices shouting, "Murder! The King is slain!" Shocked guests ran from their rooms and spoke in whispers. Who could have murdered the King?

Rumours flew through the castle like swallows – and suspicion fell on Malcolm and Donalbain, who had the most to gain from their father's death.

Malcolm and Donalbain were convinced that Macbeth was the murderer, but they did not dare to accuse him – who would believe that the hero of the battle against the Norwegians would slay his own King?

Though they knew it would be taken as proof of their guilt, Duncan's sons fled for their lives. Donalbain sailed for Ireland,

and Malcolm rode across the border into England, to put himself under the protection of the English King.

Now nothing stood between Macbeth and the throne.

He was crowned, but the crown did not
bring him the pleasure he had imagined.
His secret dream had come true, but he
was disturbed by other dreams – dreams
of what the witches had
foretold for Banquo's
descendants.

'Have I lied and
murdered to set
Banquo's spawn on
the throne?' he brooded.
'I must find a way to rid myself
of him, and his son.'

A dark plan formed in Macbeth's
mind, and he kept it a secret – even from
Lady Macbeth. Without either of them
realising, the strange force that had
compelled them to kill Duncan was slowly
driving them apart.

Macbeth held a coronation feast in the royal castle at Dunsinane. Many of the nobles who attended remarked that Macbeth's old friend, Banquo, was not present, but Macbeth laughed when they mentioned it.

"Lord Banquo and his son must have
been delayed on their way," he said
lightly. Only he knew what had delayed
them, for he had hired two murderers to
ambush them on the road.

At the height of the feast, a servant brought Macbeth a message that two men wished to see him on urgent business. Macbeth hurried to his private chambers, and found the murderers waiting there.

"Have you done what I paid you to do?" Macbeth demanded.

"Banquo is dead, my lord," one of the murderers said. "We cut his throat and threw the body into a ditch."

Macbeth sighed with relief – perhaps now he would sleep peacefully. But then he sensed something wrong: neither of the murderers would look at him, and they kept anxiously shuffling their feet.

"And his son?" said Macbeth.

The reply was shattering. "He escaped, my lord. Banquo's son still lives."

As he returned to the banqueting hall, doubts tortured Macbeth like scorpions' stings. 'Banquo's son still lives!' he thought. 'Lives to take his revenge on me, to claim the throne and father sons who will rule after him. Is there no end to the blood that must be shed before I find peace?'

As he entered the hall, Macbeth put on a false smile to hide his troubled mind; but the smile froze when he saw a hooded figure seated in his chair. "Who dares to sit in my place?" he roared.

The guests fell silent and looked bewildered: the King's chair was empty.

"Why...no one, my lord!" said Lady Macbeth, with a forced laugh. She could see that something was wrong with her husband, but she could not guess what. "The King is jesting!" she told the nobles.

"This is no jest!" barked Macbeth. He strode angrily towards the figure, then recoiled in horror as it drew back its hood.

For what he saw was Banquo – with weed tangled in his hair, and mud streaked across his face, with a deep gash in his neck that sent a stream of blood pattering onto the flagstones and haunting, glassy eyes that stared and stared.

"Get rid of him!" Macbeth screeched.

The nobles sprang to their feet, drawing their daggers, knocking over chairs and wine cups in the confusion.

"Back to your grave!" sobbed Macbeth.

Banquo smiled – there was blood in his mouth, and his teeth shone white through it, then he faded into the shadows and the torchlight.

"My lords, the King is ill," Lady Macbeth said desperately. "Leave us now, and let him rest. In the morning, he will be himself again."

"Myself?" Macbeth moaned softly to himself. "I will not be myself again until Banquo's spirit is laid to rest. Only the witches can set me free!"

* * *

The witches were seated in a huddle around a fire, over which a cauldron bubbled. In the sky above their heads a full moon sailed, casting silver light over the battlefield, still littered with unburied corpses.

The blind witch held up her crystal. Deep inside, a tiny horse and rider galloped wildly through the night. "He comes!" she cackled. "The spell is still strong!"

And Macbeth came out of the moonlight, his horse's flanks white with lathered sweat. He climbed from the saddle and was about to speak when the hook-nosed witch called out, "The King wishes to know the future!"

"It is not for the faint-hearted!" warned the bearded witch.

"I have courage enough!" Macbeth growled.

The blind witch dipped a wooden cup into the cauldron, and held it out. "Drink!" she said.

Macbeth took the cup and lifted it to his lips, shuddering as he swallowed.

Fire, and ice, and the light of the moon burned in his brain.

The blind witch's face melted like the edge of a cloud, and became the face of Duncan, his silver hair dark with blood. "Beware Macduff, the Thane of Fife!" Duncan said, and then he changed into Banquo. "No man born of a woman can harm you," Banquo said. "You will rule until Birnam Wood walks to Dunsinane."

"Then I am safe!" cried Macbeth. "No one can stop me!"

And he was alone: the witches, their cauldron and the fire had vanished.

* * *

It was the start of a fearful time. On his return to Dunsinane, Macbeth ordered that Macduff be arrested. When he heard that Macduff had fled to England to join Malcolm, Macbeth had Macduff's castle burned, and his wife and children put to death. From then on, anyone who questioned the King's commands – no matter how harsh or unjust those commands might be – was executed.

The gap between Macbeth and his wife grew wider. The guilty secret of Duncan's murder gnawed at Lady Macbeth's mind like a maggot inside an apple. She fell ill and began to walk in her sleep, dreaming that she and Macbeth were still covered with Duncan's blood. "Out, damned stain!" she croaked. "Will nothing make me clean?" Doctors could do nothing for her, and she grew weaker every day.

* * *

Then at last hope came to Macbeth's suffering subjects. Malcolm had raised an army in England and, with Macduff at his side, he marched his troops into Scotland. There the army was greeted by cheering crowds, who longed to be freed from the tyrant Macbeth.

First Glamis Castle was captured and burned, and then Malcolm's forces marched on to Dunsinane. To the despair of Macbeth's generals, he did nothing.

Each time they advised him to go to battle, he laughed and said, "I have nothing to fear until the day that Birnam Wood walks to Dunsinane."

✳ ✳ ✳

Through the windows of the throne room, Macbeth could see the distant campfires of Malcolm's army. He raised a cup of wine to them. "Fools!" he jeered. "You cannot overthrow me!"

A sound made him turn. A servant was standing at the door, wringing his hands and weeping.

"What is it?" Macbeth asked gruffly.

"The Queen, my lord," said the servant. "She is...dead."

For a long time, Macbeth was silent, remembering the early years of his marriage, when the world had seemed bright. "Life goes on, day after day, but it means nothing," he said in a cracked whisper. "It ends in despair, and darkness... and death."

Macbeth did not sleep that night. He drank cup after cup of wine, but it brought him no comfort. Only the certainty that his enemies would be defeated and that he would remain unharmed, gave him any hope.

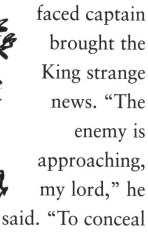

At dawn, an anxious-faced captain brought the King strange news. "The enemy is approaching, my lord," he said. "To conceal the strength of their numbers, they are hiding behind branches cut from Birnam Wood. It looks as though a forest is on the march."

"My curse upon you, witches!" howled Macbeth. "You deceived me! I have lost everything, but at least I can die like a soldier, with a sword in my hand! Go tell the servants to bring my armour!"

* * *

It was a short battle. Macbeth's army had no stomach for a fight to protect a king they now hated, and the soldiers began to surrender to Malcolm's men – first in a trickle, then in a flood.

Macbeth fought recklessly, as though he wished to be killed, but he hacked down opponent after opponent, shouting, "You were born of woman!" as he delivered the death blow.

At last, Macbeth found himself alone. He was resting against a cart, when he heard someone call his name. It was Macduff, striding through the smoke of battle, his broadsword at the ready. "I have come to avenge my wife and children!" Macduff said through clenched teeth.

"Stay back!" warned Macbeth. "I cannot be harmed by a man born of woman."

"My mother died before I was born," said Macduff, his eyes blazing with hate. "To save me, the doctor cut me from her body."

Macbeth threw back his head and laughed bitterly. He saw now that all the witches' promises had been lies, and that by believing them, he had betrayed himself. The force that had dominated him was gone, and only his courage remained. "Come then, Macduff!" he cried. "Make an end of me!"

Macduff struck off Macbeth's head with a single sweep of his sword.

＊ ＊ ＊

The head was placed on top of a spear
that had been driven into the ground
outside the gates of Dunsinane. The
victorious army cheered, then marched
away to see Malcolm crowned King.

As the sun set, three ravens flapped down
from the castle walls and fluttered around
Macbeth's head. "All hail, Macbeth!" they
cawed. "All hail! All hail!"

Out, out, brief candle.
Life's but a walking shadow, a poor player
That struts and frets his hour upon the stage,
And then is heard no more.

Macbeth; V.v.

Evil in Macbeth

Shakespeare wrote *Macbeth* in 1605, four years after James I came to the throne. King James had written a book about witchcraft, and Shakespeare wove three witches into *Macbeth,* to flatter the new monarch, who had granted Shakespeare's acting company the title of *The King's Men* in 1603.

Shakespeare's witches do not simply cast wicked spells. Their prophecies and promises play on Macbeth's mind, bringing out a long-kept secret – his ambition to be king.

The evil in the play does not come from the witches, but from Macbeth himself. Urged on by his wife, Macbeth murders the saintly King Duncan, condemns the king's sons as murderers, and is proclaimed king by the Scots noblemen.

Macbeth's dark dream has come true, but his life turns into a nightmare. To keep the throne he has his best friend murdered, and puts to death anyone who dares oppose him. The brave general has become a cruel tyrant.

In the end, Macbeth loses everything. His wife goes mad and dies, and when an English army invades Scotland his noblemen turn against him. The promises the witches made to Macbeth prove to be hollow, and he dies at the hands of Macduff, whose wife and children he had executed.

With its three witches, a ghost and a phantom dagger, *Macbeth* was the sixteenth century equivalent of a modern horror movie. But the real horror lies in the change that comes over Macbeth's character. The potential for evil, Shakespeare seems to suggest, is lurking inside us all, and we must constantly be on guard against it.

Shakespeare and the Globe Theatre

Some of Shakespeare's most famous plays were first performed at the Globe Theatre, which was built on the South Bank of the River Thames in 1599.

Going to the Globe was a different experience from going to the theatre today. The building was roughly circular in shape, but with flat sides: a little like a doughnut crossed with a fifty-pence piece. Because the Globe was an open-air theatre, plays were only put on during daylight hours in spring and summer. People paid a penny to stand in the central space and watch a play, and this part of the audience became known as 'the groundlings' because they stood on the ground. A place in the tiers of seating beneath the thatched roof, where there was a slightly better view and less chance of being rained on, cost extra.

The Elizabethans did not bath very often and the audiences at the Globe were smelly. Fine ladies and gentlemen in the more expensive seats sniffed perfume and bags of sweetly-scented herbs to cover the stink rising from the groundlings.

There were no actresses on the stage; all the female characters in Shakespeare's plays would have been acted by boys, wearing wigs and make-up. Audiences were not well-behaved. People clapped and cheered when their favourite actors came on stage; bad actors were jeered at and sometimes pelted with whatever came to hand.

Most Londoners worked hard to make a living and in their precious free time they liked to be entertained. Shakespeare understood the magic of the theatre so well that today, almost four hundred years after his death, his plays still cast a spell over the thousands of people that go to see them.

Orchard Classics
Shakespeare Stories

RETOLD BY ANDREW MATTHEWS
ILLUSTRATED BY TONY ROSS

Orchard Classics are available from all good bookshops,
or can be ordered direct from the publisher:
Orchard Books, PO BOX 29, Douglas IM99 1BQ
Credit card orders please telephone 01624 836000
or fax 01624 837033
or e-mail: bookshop@enterprise.net for details.

To order please quote title, author and ISBN
and your full name and address.
Cheques and postal orders should be
made payable to 'Bookpost plc'.
Postage and packing is FREE within the UK
(overseas customers should add £1.00 per book).

Prices and availability are subject to change.